THE WOLFSONG SERIES

The Stolen Spear

SAVIOUR PIROTTA

ILLUSTRATED BY
DAVIDE ORTU

CONTENTS

THE ISLANDS

(Now known as
the Orkneys, Scotland)

Wolf's Village

The Island of
Red Cliffs

Chapter 1
A Beached Whale

The sun had not yet risen as I stumbled bleary-eyed out of our house, closely followed by my dog, Shadow. It's my elder brother's job to look after the sheep during the night and he doesn't like it when I'm not there to take over the moment the sun comes up.

I was making sure my flint knife was secure under my belt when Shadow started barking. I looked up to see a girl running towards me. I knew her well. She was my cousin. Her family lived in a small village close to the shore where they collect a strange black stone called pumice.

'Raven,' I called.

'There's a beached whale down by Green Rock,' gasped my cousin. 'Father spotted it only just now. Mother said to let everyone in your village know before strangers get to it.'

I watched her turn and run back along the path. Then I hurried indoors along a dark, twisting corridor that led to our front door. It was so low you had to duck to get through it.

'Did you forget something?' asked my mother, peering through the smoke of the cooking fire.

'There's a whale washed up on the beach,' I said. 'Just on the other side of Green Rock.'

My father looked up from his breakfast. 'A beached whale, did you say?'

'Aye! Cousin Raven came up from the shore to tell us.'

He was on his feet in an instant. My father is a tall man and he cast a long shadow on the wall. I flinched as he spoke to me in his gruff voice.

'Go and inform the others in the village. Tell everyone to gather at the meeting place. And tell

the shaman to be there too.'

The corridor that leads to our front door connects all the houses in our village, the best one on Great Island, our home. That way we can visit each other without having to step out in the cold and rain. I ran along it now, poking my head through the open doorways.

'Father said we're all to meet outside the tool workshop. Right now.'

Our village has no official leader. We are all equal. Even Moon, the shaman who protects us from evil spirits, is not considered above others. But some people are better at certain things than others and they become temporary leaders when they are needed. My father is very good at organising crowds and it was to him that people turned as he came out of the stone corridor.

'What is the matter, Bear? Has someone tried stealing the sheep?'

'There's a beached whale down by Green Rock,' said Father. 'We must get to it before the

other villages find out about it. Bring your flint knives and axes. Bring baskets for the meat.'

A beached whale is always good news for our village, for any village really. It means plenty to eat for the next few moons. There will even be a feast around the fire with guests and storytelling. We have a very good storyteller in our village. We call him 'the keeper of the stories' because he can remember the slightest detail about people and events, and weave it into his stories. His tales keep memories of our ancestors alive.

Mother will hang great chunks of whale meat from the ceiling where it will get cooked by the smoke from the fire. It'll be a life saver in the coming winter when fresh food is scarce. The whalebone will be turned into tools and beads for necklaces.

'I'll come with you all to thank the spirit of the whale,' said Moon, 'and to offer a gift to the sea.'

He was a short fellow with a bushy beard and wild hair, both of which had turned white with age. Feathers and pierced shells dangled in his hair. His round, pale eyes had given him his name. They were full of kindness when he looked at you.

Moon lived in a house just outside the village with his son, Rain. It was bigger than anyone else's but I wouldn't want to live there myself. It's close to the underground rooms where we keep the bones of our dead ancestors.

'I'll fetch a basket for our family's share of the whale, Father,' I said.

Father scowled. 'You'll only get in the way, Wolf.'

'But, Father–' I started to argue.

Father's eyes narrowed, which meant he was getting angry. 'You know the sight of all that blood will give you bad dreams.'

This was true. The sight of dead or injured animals makes me feel terrible. It's why I never go hunting. But today I promised myself I would not be squeamish. I would earn my share of the meat.

'I was the first one in the village to get the news,' I insisted. 'I want to go with you.'

'Don't argue with me,' growled Father. 'Go and take over from your brother in the meadow. Hawk will come with us instead. Hurry up!'

'Yes, Wolf,' said the shaman kindly. 'Do as your father says.'

My ears burned with shame as I set off to the meadow where we grazed our sheep. Shadow trotted loyally behind me. He always sensed when I was upset and was as quiet as a mouse.

I know I can talk back but I hate it when Father puts me down in front of others. He would never do that to Hawk. The other children will be making snide remarks behind my back for a long time now, especially Rain. For some reason, the shaman's son doesn't like me. He takes every opportunity to push me around, although never in front of his father, who only has gentle words for me.

Weakness of any kind is frowned upon in our community. Only bravery is admired, because it helps us to survive the harsh winters and attacks from our enemies.

I pray to the spirits every day to make me brave. I especially pray to the spirit of the wolf because I am named after him. We of the stone village believe our names affect the way we live. My father's parents called him Bear because they hoped he would grow up to be as fierce as one.

Their wish came true because my father has a wild temper and lashes out at people when he gets angry.

I got my name because a shadow of a wolf fell across our doorway the moment I was born. My mother says it was almost like the wolf had come to pay his respects. It was a sign from the spirits, although she had no idea what it meant.

I pushed the thoughts of names and their meanings aside as I got to our grazing field. My brother, Hawk, smiled when he saw me and Shadow approaching.

'I'm so glad to see you,' he said. 'Can't wait to tuck into a warm breakfast when I get home.'

'You'll not want to waste time on breakfast when you hear this,' I said. 'There's a beached whale down by Green Rock. Father wants you to go help strip it.'

Hawk's face lit up at the news. 'Great! I could do with a bit of action after sitting here all night. Don't let the fire go out, Wolf. I don't want to have to light another one tonight. And make sure you watch the lambs carefully: I spotted an eagle earlier.'

'I'll keep an eye out for it,' I promised.

Shadow and I settled down to wait out the long day. In the distance, I could hear the rest of the village making its way down to the beach. Then all was quiet. The sun rose higher and I lay back in the grass to watch the sky. I often do that, just look up at the sky and wonder what lies hidden behind that ceiling of bright blue. I know that every rock on our island, every animal and tree has its own spirit that must be kept happy at all times. Hidden spirits control the earth, the sea and the sky.

Was the sky spirit looking down at me right now? I hoped so, for I have always felt closer to the sky spirit than any other.

Some time later I heard the villagers coming back from the beach. They sounded happy and the women were singing. That made me feel miserable all over again. How I wished I had been allowed to go with them.

I ate my lunch, feeding Shadow most of it for sadness makes me lose my appetite. Then I walked around the meadow, making sure the lambs had not wandered off. After that there was nothing else to do, except look at the sky some more.

The hot sun must have lulled me to sleep because the next thing I knew, Shadow was barking furiously. I sat up, hastily wiping my face. The sun was setting. I had slept for ages. To my horror, I could hear a terrified bleating. An eagle had snatched one of the lambs!

I scrambled to my feet, trying hard not to panic. What would Hawk do in this situation? *Ha*, snickered a little voice inside my head, *Hawk would never fall asleep when he's looking after the sheep. And you promised him you'd watch out for the eagle too…*

Shadow had set off after the bird, still barking

madly. It ignored him and swooped higher. Within moments, it was just a speck in the sky.

I know that eagles are higher beings and that their needs must be met but I felt sorry for the poor lamb, and angry with myself for not protecting it. I was going to be in a lot of trouble when Father found out he had one less lamb to barter with when traders came to the village.

What I didn't realise was that this trouble would set me off on an adventure that would change my entire life.

Chapter 2
Trapped!

I trudged home slowly, dreading the inevitable argument with my father. Hawk had been very understanding when I told him what had happened. My father would not be so forgiving.

The village was already preparing for the big feast when I got back. Smoke rose in wispy columns from the cooking holes in the roofs of the houses. A delicious smell filled the corridors.

Mother was hanging meat above the fire as I ducked through the doorway. 'Did you have a good day?'

'An eagle carried off one of the lambs,' I forced myself to say.

My mother groaned but my father said nothing. He had his back to me and I saw it stiffen with fury.

'Wolf,' said Mother. 'We were counting on that lamb to pay for grain and new cloth. The traders arrive tomorrow. What were you doing while the eagle picked off the lamb?'

'I… I fell asleep.'

'Oh, Wolf. How could you?'

The way Mother looked at me hurt more than any words. I could see the disappointment in her eyes. Father turned suddenly. His eyes were blazing but he didn't look directly at me.

'Your son brings shame on this family,' he growled at my mother. Then he marched out of the house, the fire spreading his shadow across the ceiling as he made for the door.

'You all think I'm a weakling,' I snapped at Mother, 'but I'll make up for my mistake. You'll have something to barter with when traders come tomorrow.'

I grabbed a basket off the floor.

'Where are you going with that?' Mother asked.

'Out.'

'Wolf, it's dark outside.'

I didn't reply. Father was not the only one who could hurt with his silence. Instead I whistled for Shadow, who followed me along the stone corridor. I hurried down the same path my cousin Raven had taken in the morning. I was heading for the shore. As Mother said, it was dark, the time for lost spirits to creep out of their hiding places.

But I didn't care. I had a clever plan to make up for the lost lamb. I would fill my basket with auk eggs, which are very good for bartering.

Auks are big, lumbering birds who live on the rocky shores of our island. They have small wings which keep them from flying. Their eggs have speckled shells and are delicious when roasted in smoking peat.

They are hard to find but I had discovered a

secret auk nesting place. It was dangerous to get
to, at the far end of the bay some distance from
our village, and hidden behind a row of large,
jagged rocks that I call the Shark's Teeth. I always
pray to their spirits when I walk past them, to stop
them from toppling over me.

A bright moon had risen by the time I reached
the shore. The whale's enormous skeleton still lay
on the shingle, surrounded by birds who were
busy pecking at the bones. I kept away from it, in
case its confused spirit was still around.

With Shadow growling softly at my heels, I
picked my way along the beach and round a

headland. The rocky ground here was slippery with seaweed and I had to tread carefully as I scrambled up to the higher ground where the auks nested.

Auks live in pairs and rear only one chick at a time. The mother lays the egg on bare rock. One parent stays behind to protect it while the other hunts for food in the sea. Only very rarely do both birds stray from the egg, leaving it unguarded, so I knew I had to be patient if I were to collect any. I wedged myself behind a large rock which stank of seaweed and settled down for a long night.

I have no idea how much time passed as I lay

in wait, darting out every time a nest was left unguarded. But at last my basket was full.

'Let's get home,' I said to Shadow. 'I'm frozen stiff.' Shadow had been very patient, not even growling when the auks waddled right up to our hiding place looking for their missing eggs.

We scrambled down the rocks, only to get a nasty surprise when we came to the far end of the Shark's Teeth. The tide was coming in. Already the pebbly shore had disappeared under a blanket of hissing, foaming water. Our way forward was cut off.

'We'll have to go back to the auks' nesting ground,' I said to Shadow. 'We'll wait there until the tide goes out.'

We made our way back along the Shark's Teeth, the basket of eggs now feeling heavy in my arms. But by the time we got to the other end, the higher rock was half under water too. There was no way of getting up to the auks' nesting ground. We were trapped on the headland between the rising water and the sheer cliff behind us.

'Oh, Shadow,' I cried. 'What are we going to do?'

I begged the spirit of the sea to keep me from harm as the water rose higher, seeping into my furry shoes. I don't think he was listening. Shadow barked furiously at the waves, as if to scare them back. Then he looked up and barked ferociously, his tail wagging to and fro. I followed his gaze – and realised the sea spirit might have heard my prayers after all.

There was a head poking out of a hole in the cliff.

Chapter 3
A Stranger to the Rescue

'Help,' I shouted. 'We're trapped!'

'Don't worry,' came back the reply above the sound of rushing water. 'I've got a rope with me. You can climb up.'

Shadow yapped at the tufty end of the rope as it came slowly down until it bumped against his nose.

'Tie up your dog first,' shouted the figure at the hole. 'I'll haul him up.'

By now I was knee deep in seawater and my legs were so cold I couldn't feel them. With trembling fingers, I wrapped the rope around Shadow's middle and knotted it tight under his

belly. He gave my nose a friendly lick as the stranger hauled him up.

It felt like ages before the rope came down again. I used the time to tie the basket securely around my neck. I'd risked my life to find those eggs and I was not going to lose them if I could help it.

I grabbed the end of the rope, wrapped it twice around my wrist and began hauling myself up. I am not known among my people for having strong arms and the going was tough. My feet slipped on the wet cliff-face but step by step I advanced towards the hole.

A thick sea-mist had blown in and I swear I could see tendrils of fog reaching out like skeletal fingers. Were the spirits trying to pull me back into the sea, as punishment for stealing the auk eggs? I forced myself to look away, to keep my eyes on Shadow who was waiting for me, and the hooded face of my rescuer reaching out to pull me to safety.

As I clambered into the hole, she grinned. The dark circle around her face wasn't a hood. It was a wild mop of hair, as dark as burnt wood. Her green eyes flashed at me.

'Thank the spirits your dog's barking woke me up.'

'Yes, thank you,' I said. 'Shadow and I would both have drowned if you hadn't come to our rescue.'

Shadow licked her knee to show he agreed with me. The girl was dressed in a long tunic made of hide and thick boots. A fur cloak flapped at her back. A large flint knife was tucked under her belt.

'How did you discover this tunnel?' I asked. 'I know this shore like the back of my hand and I never even knew it existed.'

'I'm good at finding tunnels,' she replied. 'My name should be Rabbit.'

I laughed at her joke. 'So what is your name?'

'Crow! What's yours?'

'Wolf. And my dog is called Shadow.'

'Pleased to meet you both,' said Crow, rubbing Shadow's back. My dog had taken to her right away and leapt up to lick her face.

'What were you doing in this tunnel?' I asked.

'I'm travelling,' said Crow. 'I want to see if I can survive without the help of my father and my people. I always spend the night in a tunnel if I can. It's good shelter, and easier to defend yourself in an attack.'

'And you are out of sight from night-spirits too,' I added, my voice falling to a whisper. 'It is my belief that some of them can swallow people whole.'

Crow shrugged, still playing with Shadow. She didn't seem at all worried about night-spirits.

I checked the eggs in my basket. Surprisingly, none were broken.

'I should offer one of these to the sea, for allowing me to live,' I said. 'Then you must come to my house for something to eat. I'm sure my parents would be grateful to you for saving my life, even if I'm not as useful as my brother Hawk.'

I hurled one of the eggs into the sea and watched it disappear in the foam. Then I hurried after Crow towards the other end of the tunnel.

Chapter 4
The Bead Necklace

Crow told me a lot about herself as we hurried back to my village. Her mother had died while giving birth to her. She was an only child and lived with her father, a village chief.

Her people made their home on an island far away, a place she called Seal Island. She said it was a very different island from ours, with trees that grew densely together. Our island is bare compared to hers, even though it's much bigger.

Like us, Crow's people grew crops and kept animals. They also cured hides and smoked meat for the winter and told stories around the fire.

Shadow trotted obediently at our heels.

'He's a loyal dog,' said Crow. 'Did you get him when he was a newborn puppy?'

'No,' I said. 'I'm not sure where he came from. He appeared out of the mist one day, while I was looking after the sheep. There'd been a terrific storm with lightning that hit a nearby tree. I was petrified and screamed for the good spirits to help me. A moment later I saw a shadow moving through the mist, and then two yellow eyes. It was a dog. He followed me home and has never left my side since.'

'Like a shadow,' said Crow.

I nodded.

'How mysterious,' said Crow. 'He's your guardian, a protector.'

The sun had not yet risen as we reached the village but the corridors between the houses were already humming with activity.

'Our houses are not connected to each other like this,' observed Crow. 'We have to go out in the cold if we need anything, or if we want to visit neighbours.'

The door to our house had already been opened for the day so I marched right in.

'Here are enough eggs for all of us, and to barter with,' I announced, placing the basket on the stone shelves where we kept our food and precious possessions. 'I hope the traders have not been yet.'

There was no sign of Father.

'Thank the spirits you're home safe and sound, Wolf,' said Mother. 'Your father and I were worried sick about you. You could easily have come to grief on such a wild night. Your father is out looking for you.'

'I did come to grief,' I replied. 'But this girl saved my life, and Shadow's too. Her name is Crow.'

My mother looked at Crow who was hanging back in the doorway waiting for my mother's invitation to come in.

'Welcome to our house. We are indebted to

you,' said my mother. 'Warm yourself by the fire for a few moments while I get you both something to eat. You can have it on your way to the pastures. Wolf, you must hurry. Your brother is just as worried about you as your father and I.'

She gave us milk to drink while she wrapped some leftovers from last night's feast in a piece of cloth and handed them to me. I was about to duck back through the doorway when Mother said, 'Wait.'

She reached to the back of the stone shelves where there was a hard-to-see cubby hole. 'Here, child,' she said to Crow, pulling out a bead necklace. 'It's all I have to give you. My own mother, Wolf's grandmother who passed away a long time ago, carved the beads herself from bone. Keep it safe. It will protect you.'

The necklace was Mother's only treasure. Her own mother, who died before I was born, had given it to her on her wedding day. The knuckles were painted a bright blue, a symbol of the sky and therefore protection. Mother only wore it on very special occasions.

Crow put it carefully round her neck. 'Thank you,' she said. 'Seeing you in your nice, warm home has reminded me how much I miss my own family. I have been travelling for many moons. Perhaps it is time to return to my own island.'

She fingered the beads. 'These will bring good fortune to my father too.'

Shadow growled his special growl which was a warning that Father was coming. I dived out of the front door, nearly banging my head, and Crow followed.

Much to my dismay, we were not quick enough. We bumped into Father at the end of the corridor. I cringed, expecting a growl of anger at my disappearance, but he looked at me and I could see the relief in his eyes.

'Hurry up,' he said. 'Hawk will want to know you're safe.'

'You'll like Hawk,' I said to Crow on our way to the meadow. 'All the girls like him.'

Crow nodded at the shaman's house. We could hear music coming from inside. The holy man was playing his bone flute. Behind the house rose a grassy hill.

'Is that a burial mound?' asked Crow.

'Yes,' I said. 'We bury our most important

people in it.'

'We have one like it at home,' said Crow.

'Do you keep the door to it always closed too?' I asked. 'We only open ours on the days we take the skeletons out to honour and respect them. All the other days, the dead lie peacefully with their belongings.

'There is one special skeleton we believe has been in there for over a hundred years. He was an ancient healer, known for his ability to cure any sickness.'

'I don't think our burial mound has any special people buried in it,' said Crow. 'But we still consider it a sacred place. To be honest, I find it a bit scary.'

'Our healer's spear is still full of magic. It protects our village. There are symbols and images of dolphins and deer carved in the shaft. The spearhead is made of chert, a stone you can only find close to our village.'

Crow shivered and pulled her fur cloak tighter

against her shoulders. 'Let's change the subject,' she said.

Shadow whined deep in his throat.

Crow tickled the spot between his ears. 'Is he afraid of the dead too?'

'Shadow's not afraid of anything,' I said proudly. 'He has picked up the scent of someone he doesn't like.'

As I spoke, the door to the shaman's house opened and Rain strode out. I imagine Rain's parents called him that because they hoped he would bring life and health to everyone he met. I think Flood would have been a more suitable name, because he caused disaster wherever he went. He was a very tall boy, with a spotty face and the same fiery red hair that his father used to have. His fists were always bunched up, ready for a fight. He was always picking on me and I disliked him intensely.

'So who's this you're dragging around with you today?' he asked, ogling Crow.

'A friend,' I said.

'Didn't know you had any,' sneered Rain. 'Never seen her before. Are you sure she's not a spy for some hostile tribe, or a thief?'

'Crow is braver than you'll ever be,' I argued, before she pulled me back.

'Leave him be, Wolf,' said Crow. 'He's a bully.'

Rain spat at my feet. 'Who do you think you are, bringing total strangers to our village? I'm going to tell my father about you, and when I am shaman I shall ban all strangers like her from the village.'

Chapter 5
Skeletons

'I hate Rain,' I fumed as Crow and I continued towards the pastures.

'Don't waste another thought on him,' said Crow. 'It's going to be a warm, sunny day. Let's enjoy it. I want to remember your island forever.'

'Is your home, Seal Island, very far away?' I asked.

'It took me three seasons to get here,' replied Crow. 'But that's because I took time off to explore.'

I spotted Hawk counting the sheep. 'There's my elder brother,' I said.

Hawk breathed a huge sigh of relief when he

saw me. 'Have you been home yet?' he asked. 'Father's been out looking for you.'

'He knows I'm safe,' I replied.

Hawk smiled at Crow. 'Is this a friend of yours?'

'Yes,' I replied. 'She saved my life.'

'Our family is grateful to you,' Hawk said to Crow. 'Are you from the next village on the island?'

'I'm from another island completely,' answered Crow. 'As I was saying to Wolf, it took me three seasons to reach your island.'

'Well, thank you for saving Wolf, wherever you come from,' said Hawk. 'I'm sure my parents will tell me all about it over breakfast.'

When Hawk left, leaving me once more in charge of the sheep, I shared out the whale meat and told Crow some stories about our village.

'You are very good at telling tales,' said Crow. 'Even better than the storyteller in our village. Do you hope to become your people's keeper of memories when you grow up?'

'I don't know what I want to be,' I admitted. 'I'm no good at fishing or hunting. And much as I like planting seeds and watching them come to life, I suspect I won't make a good farmer either.'

'Perhaps the spirits will show you what life-path to take,' said Crow kindly.

'I beg them to show me every night. I ask the sun too, because I know he is the source of all life and knowledge. But so far I have not received any answers. Do you know what you want to be when you grow up?'

'As a chief's daughter, I want to become the best warrior among my people,' said Crow. 'I shall make sure no one on my island ever goes to bed afraid of an enemy attack.'

We spent a lovely morning talking about things I'd never discussed with anyone before, not just about my future, but about my beliefs, my fears and regrets too. It's amazing how talking to someone who knows how to listen helps you sort out your thoughts.

When it was time for Crow to leave, Shadow and I watched her making her way down to the shore where she had hidden her boat.

'I do wish we'd meet her again, Shadow,' I said. 'I feel Crow and I could be best friends.'

We watched her boat head out to the wide, open sea. I've heard that some tribes who live in the lands beyond the sea travel far distances by boat. Like us, they make them out of tree branches and animal hides. But our boats are not so good and tend to start taking in water after a while.

In any case, our people mistrust the sea. They cannot see the end of it and that makes them afraid of it. What lies at the other end? The home of the sun? Other peoples, perhaps wilder and fiercer than us? People who might one day come and attack us?

As for me, I have never been afraid of the sea. When the sun is setting, I gaze at the golden path it makes on the water and wonder if one day I'll find a way to walk on it, and where it would take me.

A useless yet powerful dream, I know, but I could never help myself.

Autumn turned to winter, bringing ice and snow. Sometimes it seemed the sun never came up at all. We lived in darkness.

The sea pounded the rocky shore for days on end. The small lake close to our village froze, making it impossible to fish, and we were glad

Mother had smoked some of the whale meat. Without it we would have starved.

But gradually the days grew longer, the air warmer. Spring brought with it much hard work but also much pleasure. There were new lambs and calves to look after. Fields were tilled, the hard soil broken up with wooden ploughs. We planted new crops, went fishing in both the lake and the sea. Now we could enjoy fresh food again and play out in the sunshine after our work was done.

Soon we were all preparing for a very important event. Midsummer! It's the longest day of the year. The sun rises to the highest pinnacle in the sky, filling the world with its power and energy. It's a time for cleaning and repairing our houses, a time for celebration, for feasting and dancing, but also for making sure that we will have a good harvest.

We do that by honouring our dead ancestors in the hope that their wisdom and experience will live on through us.

The ceremony is a grim one that has been known to give children nightmares. The burial mound outside the village is opened and the first ray of the morning sun is allowed to shine inside. The skeletons of the most important people in the village are brought out to enjoy the light once again. We take this opportunity to show their spirits how much we respect them. We talk to them as if they were still alive, and the shaman receives the answers on our behalf. The dead tell us when to plant our seeds, when to expect storms and where to hunt for the biggest game.

The hunters in the village had caught a wild boar for the feast. A bonfire was lit in the meeting place and we danced around it while

the meat cooked, filling the air with a mouth-watering smell and the shaman thanked the spirit of the boar for giving us its strength and life.

After the feast, we carried flaming torches to the burial mound. We wore masks, to make us all look fiercer and wiser. Shadow growled softly at the strange, unsmiling faces. He whined when Father and the axe maker helped the shaman open the door to the burial mound. I didn't think he was scared but I curled my arms around him just the same.

As the sky grew lighter, we put out our torches. The sun peeped over the edge of the world, turning the sea a dazzling yellow. Its first ray reached across the water and inside the burial mound.

'Come with me,' said the shaman to Father and the axe maker.

The three of them stole silently through the open door and we heard the sound of the shaman's eerie singing as he communicated with the spirits.

A few moments later, the three men came back out. They were carrying a skeleton laid out on a wooden plank, which they set down on a stone altar.

'Behold the ancient hunter, whose arrows never failed to miss their mark,' said the shaman in a loud voice. 'The best hunter our village has ever known. He has often spoken to me in my dreams, helping me find new hunting grounds. Come, pay your respects that his spirit might help us catch enough prey to last us through the coming winter.'

The crowd jostled forward but I hung back, still holding Shadow tight in my arms. If I'm honest, skulls and skeletons frighten me as much as bleeding wounds. I did not want to look at the dead hunter.

Rain looked back at me. 'Too scared to look, Wolfie boy?'

'No.'

'Then what's stopping you from getting closer? Come on, have a good look, or will you get nightmares?'

'You have a good stare if you want,' I snapped.

Father, the shaman and the axe maker carried the skeleton back into the burial mound and came back with another.

'Now behold the ancient healer,' said the shaman. 'He who has lain in the dust for many a season but whose power still protects us all from sickness and death.'

The women surged forward, their wailing

voices rising in the morning air.

'Oh great healer, protect our families. Keep harm away from us and we will keep your memory alive forever.'

Then a piercing scream cut the wailing short. One of the women pointed to the healer's skeleton. 'Look, it's gone. It's missing. The sacred spear has been stolen!'

Chapter 6
The Stolen Spear

The meeting place was packed. Even the people from the fishing village on the shore had come. They all sat on the hard earth, looking up expectantly at the shaman.

Everyone was troubled. Just breaking into a burial ground, even if you touched nothing, was an insult to the spirits. Actually stealing from the dead was a sure way of attracting a curse, not only for the thief but also for the community in charge of the tomb.

The shaman, who had called the gathering, quietened everyone down.

'Please do not panic. Perhaps the spear just fell

out of the healer's hands,' he said. 'Bear and the axe maker are having a good look round the tomb as we speak. They might find it lying in the dust.'

My father and the axe man soon arrived.

'I'm afraid there's no sign of the spear,' he said, his eyes bright with the fury I knew and feared. 'We looked everywhere.'

An angry murmur went through the crowd. 'If it isn't there, then it *was* stolen,' shouted one of our neighbours.

She started keening at the top of her voice and the other women joined her.

'Our children will be cursed,' she cried, 'and the spirit of the healer whose spear was stolen will not protect us from illness anymore.'

'We still don't know for sure that it was stolen,' said the shaman, hoping to calm everyone down.

Rain, who had been sitting at the front of the crowd with his friends, jumped to his feet.

'Well, I for one think we should get to the bottom of this.' He signalled to his friends.

'Are you coming?'

'I warn you not to enter the burial place without my permission,' said his father.

'We don't need to go inside,' replied Rain. 'Thieves *always* leave clues outside.'

He marched off with his friends. The rest of the crowd followed, including me. Despite the summer, the sky had clouded over and it looked like it was going to rain.

We reached the burial mound, where Father and the axe maker had already put the stone door back in place.

From a distance, the mound had always looked like an ordinary green hill, not much different from all the other hills in the countryside. But now, seeing it up close, I could tell it was actually different in many little ways. Spooky even. No flowers grew on it. There were no rabbit holes, which are everywhere at this time of year. And no birds pecked around the grass looking for food. Perhaps the spirits that lay beneath had scared them away.

I shivered as I followed the crowd round the base of the mound and Shadow whined, as if afraid of something. Rain stopped near a prickly gorse bush.

'Look,' he said, moving the branches aside with his boot. 'There's a hole here. A tunnel. The thief must have dug his way into the mound.'

The rest gathered round, eager to have a look.

'And look, just as I expected. A clue.'

He bent down and picked something off the ground. It was a large bead, painted a bright blue.

'Here's another one,' cried one of his friends, 'and there are more under the bush.'

He held up the beads for everyone to see.

'I've seen these before,' said Rain. 'On a necklace.'

He glared at me with a twisted grin on his lips. 'Your friend was wearing it when you showed her round the village, wasn't she? She was a spy, just as I suspected. You revealed our secrets to a stranger and she came back to steal the healer's spear. Now we are doomed, all because of *you*.'

My blood turned to ice as everyone in the crowd turned to me.

'Why would she do that?' I argued weakly.

'We are a powerful and well-known village,'

replied an old man who was considered the best farmer on the island. 'We attract the blessing of the spirits. We are known for our skills at fishing and hunting.'

He pushed his way to the front of the crowd so everyone could see him. 'Our crops, the tools and weapons we make, even our jewellery, fetch more at bartering than any other.

Perhaps your friend's people are jealous. They want to be the best village themselves. And they might soon be. Without the protection of the sacred spear, our village will soon come to harm, mark my word.'

I could feel a wave of hot anger coming off the crowd towards me. Shadow, still in my arms, whimpered sadly. He too could feel their rage.

The farmer's words made me feel dreadful. To think that my hasty actions had brought danger to our community. I looked from Mother to the shaman, hoping they would say something to defend me. But I could see only hurt and worry in their eyes.

By now it had started to rain.

'I am sorry if I have betrayed my own people,' I said loudly, thankful for the rain that was hiding my shameful tears. 'But I shall make up for my mistake. I will go off in search of the thief and when I return, I swear I shall bring the stolen spear back with me.'

Chapter 7
A Wicker Skiff and a Driftwood Oar

The next few days were strange and sad ones. Everyone in the village shunned me, turning their backs on me whenever I walked past. The only people who talked to me were the shaman and my family, especially Hawk who could see what I was going through.

The other children in the village spat at my feet every time they saw me. Not that I spent much time in the village. I was determined to start on my journey as soon as possible.

I found an old fisherman who was willing to help me build my own boat in exchange for help with his night-time fishing. My father had found an orphan to look after the sheep instead of me. Not because he didn't trust me anymore but because Rain and his friends kept turning up to throw stones and insults at me, and he was worried they might injure me or the lambs.

That left me free to build the boat. I made it out of wicker and dried animal skins. The cane for the wicker I cut myself from the shores of the lake near the village. The hides I bartered off the fisherman's wife, paying her with wild rabbits and auk eggs. I collected the eggs myself, but Hawk trapped the rabbits in his spare time for me. I couldn't thank him enough.

The fisherman showed me how to soak the canes in water until I could bend them in any shape I needed to form the skeleton of my skiff. He taught me how to lash them together with strong twine, covering the knots in hot tar to protect them from wear and tear. I stretched the hides over them, tight enough to stitch around the wooden frame. My fingers were always bleeding by the end of the day but I would not stop. I wanted to start my journey before the summer ended.

'How will you find your friend?' the shaman asked me one night.

'She is not my friend,' I snapped. 'Friends don't use each other like that. She tricked me.'

The shaman was silent for a few moments. Then he said, 'Do you know where she lives?'

'She said her home was on Seal Island and that it took her three seasons to get here, on account that she stopped to hunt and explore. But that might have been a lie, of course.'

'You have no choice but to look for her there first,' said the shaman. 'I visited the island with my own father a good many moons ago and can tell you how to get there. It will not take you three seasons but many a long day nonetheless. You will need to travel south, across a wild sea and often stormy sea. Now listen to me carefully and make sure you remember what I tell you.

'When you paddle out of our bay you must skirt the shore, always keeping it to your left, until you come to a place where a huge rock rises out of the ground like a giant spear. There, you must look out across the open sea. If the air is clear you will see a thin green line on the horizon. They are the shores of Seal Island, which is thick with trees and vegetation. Paddle towards it.'

I tried to take in everything the shaman was telling me, hoping against hope the spirits would guide me if I got lost.

'Be careful crossing the sea,' warned the shaman. 'There are strong currents there that might sweep you off course to another island. The Island of Red Cliffs.'

I sat in silence, going over the shaman's directions in my head.

'You shall go with my blessing,' he said after a while. 'A great injustice has been done to you. Your friendship and kindness have been abused. But I believe that this is the work of the spirits.

They are testing you. Embark on your adventure with hope and courage and it will be the making of you. Now go and spend the evening with your loved ones. I will wait for you on the shore tomorrow at dawn.'

Hiding my skiff behind a rock, I returned home for one last meal with my family. Mother had prepared stewed vegetables, which we ate round the fire.

'I've packed you some dried meat and extra furs,' said Mother, ladling out the food.

'Those furs are too flimsy for a sea journey,' cut in Father. He went to the clothes chest and came back with his best cloak, the one he'd inherited from his own father. 'Take this. Your grandfather would have wanted you to have it. His spirit will be with you to protect you and bring you back home safely.'

His unexpected kindness left me speechless. I wrapped the cloak around my shoulders, enjoying its warmth. 'Thank… you,' I stammered.

Hawk handed me two fire-making stones and a pouch full of dried grass. 'Make sure these don't get wet. You'll need them to light a fire.'

I put them in my bag gratefully. I hadn't even thought of taking fire-making stones with me.

Hawk hugged me closely. 'Be brave, brother. And most of all be kind to yourself. We shall pray to the spirits until you come back home safely to us.'

I didn't sleep at all that night and dawn found me and Shadow making our way down to the shore. The shaman was waiting for me as he'd promised.

He took my oar, which I had carved out of driftwood and hardened in the coals of a dying fire. Holding it up to the reddening sky, he closed his eyes and started singing.

There are playful songs that children sing when they are playing. There are soft, calming songs mothers sing to their babies before they go to sleep, and rowdy songs farmers bellow when they

are working in the fields. But the shaman's song was very different. It was full of magic and power, a song that spoke directly to the hidden spirits. I called it the Moonsong, after the shaman himself.

The first rays of the sun shone on the oar and, for a moment, made the blade glow like fire. The shaman opened his eyes and handed it back to me.

'There,' he said. 'It is now filled with the power of the spirits. It shall guide you home safely.'

The sun's rays had stretched across the sea to form the usual flame-coloured pathway by the time Shadow and I set out. I threw my bone cloak pin into the water as a gift to the spirits of the sea. It would protect my boat against storms and underwater monsters. On the shore, the shaman raised his hand in one last blessing and I waved back.

Now that I was out on the sea, my sadness and fears were replaced with a great excitement. Only the shaman had set out on a long journey from our island before, and that was a very long time ago. In a strange way, my dream had come true. I was going out into the big wide world.

Shadow climbed onto my lap and I kissed the top of his head. 'I am glad you are with me,' I said.

He looked up at me and I could see the morning sun reflected in his eyes. It made them sparkle like stars when the night sky is very clear. I only had a moment to gaze at them, then he turned his head and the magic was gone.

Chapter 8
A Violent Storm

I travelled close along the coast of Great Island, always keeping it to the left like the shaman had told me.

My arms felt like they'd fall off with all the paddling and it was freezing cold. I was wrapped up in my grandfather's cloak, with furry gloves, boots and a hat but my bones still felt like ice inside me. Thank the spirits it was not winter because I'm sure then I would have frozen solid.

After a while the skiff started taking in water. Alarmed, I rowed ashore and inspected it closely. Some stitching had come undone, making two of the skins come slightly apart. I repaired it with an awl and string I had brought with me.

By the time Shadow and I got back into the skiff, the sun had reached the middle of the sky. I paddled on but soon I could feel the wind rising. The sea turned choppy. It was going to rain.

I had no choice but to get back on shore again. I'd hardly dragged the skiff to safety behind a huge rock before the skies opened. With nowhere to shelter, Shadow and I were soaked to the skin. I prayed to the spirits until the rain stopped and I could use Hawk's fire-making stones to light a fire.

My mother had been very generous with her gift of dried meat but I wanted to keep that for emergencies. So I feasted on an enormous crab that I found in a rock pool. I cooked it by poking it deep into the embers of the fire like I had seen Mother do at home.

In the morning, I found a spring and refilled my goatskin before getting back into the skiff. Shadow settled at the prow again and we set off.

The shoreline to my left changed like the pictures you see in your head when you listen to a good story. Sometimes it was rocky, sometimes sandy with stone altars at the water's edge. I kept away from these places where people had offered sacrifice. Who knew whether the locals were dangerous or not?

At last we came to the strange rock the shaman had described. It really did look like a giant spear stuck in the ground. This was the southern tip of Great Island. I looked out across the vast expanse of sea. In the distance I could make out a thin green line, like a piece of string stretched along the edge of the ocean.

'That's it, Shadow,' I said. 'Our destination. Seal Island.'

I turned the boat towards it, my blood thudding in my veins with excitement. But only a few moments out on the open sea, the wind snatched the paddle straight out of my hands. My sacred paddle which the shaman had blessed, assuring me a safe return to my island, went flying into the water.

Before I even had time to think, Shadow dived in after it. He dragged it back to the skiff in his mouth, fighting the current which was doing its best to sweep him the other way. I hauled him in, thanking the spirits for sending me such a brave guardian. Poor Shadow was shaking with the cold, so I rubbed him down with the fur blanket to warm him up.

'You are a hero,' I said. 'We'd have been lost without the paddle. Here's some whale meat as a reward.'

While Shadow chewed happily away, I tied the paddle to the wrist on my right hand with a strip of leather. That way it would never get away from me again.

Sadly, it seemed I had some kind of curse on me. Without warning, the wind grew much stronger and the currents started to pull the skiff sideways. I paddled with every bit of strength in me but even so, the skiff seemed to make hardly any progress. The waves tossed it about like a leaf in a gully and before I knew it, Shadow and I were sitting in a hand span of seawater.

I started scooping it out with my hands. But the moment it seemed like we were saved, another wave would slosh over the edge of the skiff and fill it again.

In the end, I gave up and concentrated on paddling. The sun set behind a bank of newly-formed clouds. The moon rose but I could hardly see it. I was paddling in near-darkness.

'Spirits of the wind and sea, guardians of the waves, please help me,' I shouted at the top of my voice. Shadow howled along with me.

As if to mock us, there was a deafening crack of thunder and a storm broke out. Almost immediately, the skiff was full right to the brim with rain. Then a giant wave hurled it straight towards the sky. I grabbed Shadow and held onto the side.

We landed, screaming and howling, in what looked like a valley of foaming, churning waves only to be thrown up again and again. Freezing water flew into my eyes and mouth. I could hear the shrieking of gulls above the storm. They sounded like wild spirits, mocking us.

I have no idea how long the nightmare lasted but there was a moment when I thought I glimpsed red cliffs in the moonlight. Then another wave hit us from below, sending us hurtling up towards the sky.

I remember seeing Shadow plunging towards the sea below me. And then everything went dark.

Chapter 9
The Island of Red Cliffs

The morning sun was shining directly in my eyes. I had a throbbing pain in my head but I could feel soft sand under me. The storm had tossed me onto a beach.

I sat up slowly and looked around. There was no sign of either the skiff or Shadow. I thought of my trusted dog plummeting towards the roaring waves, and I feared deep in my heart he had perished at sea.

I screamed at the sea, which was now calmly lapping at the shore as if the storm had never happened. How dare the spirits take my only friend? How could they force me to continue this dangerous journey on my own? I might be able to build a new skiff but how could I go on without Shadow to protect me?

My screaming attracted attention and I soon heard shouting. I turned to see a man and a boy walking towards me. For a moment I thought they might be angry with me but there was no fury in their eyes. They were both dressed in fur tunics and leggings but their muscled arms were bare. The older man had a grey shaggy beard and leaned on a stick.

As they came closer I could see they were probably father and son. They had the same pale green eyes and thin lips.

'Were you washed up on shore by the storm?' the boy asked. He spoke my language but with a broad accent.

'Yes,' I replied. 'I am lucky to be alive. Sadly my trusted dog… he didn't make it. I lost my boat too.'

I looked around, desperately hoping to see

Shadow bounding towards me but I knew it was useless.

'Where do you come from?' said the boy.

'Great Island,' I said. 'I was on my way to Seal Island when I got caught in the storm.'

'Well, the storm has blown you off course,' said the boy. 'You are on the Island of Red Cliffs.'

'You must get out of those wet furs before you freeze to death,' said the older man. 'My son, Rock, will lend you some of his while yours dry by the fire. Come with us, our farm is in a valley behind the cliff. Ma will give you some hot food too.'

Thankful for their kindness, I followed them up a steep path and onto a rocky plateau sheltered with low-lying trees. We descended into a valley where the trees had been cleared to make fields. It was nearly harvest time and barley rippled in the wind.

The farmer's house was surrounded by open land where pigs rooted around an enormous rubbish heap. It was very different from my house on Great Island, which was built of stone and roofed with grass. This one had white walls, which I later learnt were woven out of tree branches and covered in hardened mud. The roof was made of dried twigs. Behind it, I could see another building. I supposed it must be a storeroom.

A woman with grey hair and a wrinkled face was sitting at a fire pit outside the farmhouse.

'This is Ma,' said Rock. 'She's cooking barley porridge and snails. But come inside and change into dry clothes before we eat.'

'My name is Wolf, by the way,' I said.

Ma nodded. 'Welcome, Wolf. The food will be ready soon.'

She gave me a toothy smile as I followed Rock into the house. I heard her talking with her husband while I changed from my wet furs into dry, clean ones.

'I'm sorry these clothes are a bit tatty,' said

Rock, 'but they're the only spare ones I have.'

'I don't mind,' I said. 'At least they're dry and warm.'

Back outside, Ma had hung up my wet furs close to the fire pit. She asked me to sit down and handed me a bowl of porridge. Pa, the older man, passed me a wooden spoon.

'Eat before it gets cold,' said Ma, her face all sweaty from the fire.

I tucked in hungrily. The porridge was thick and hot, just what I needed to warm me up. Pa and Rock picked at the roasted snails.

'Do you have porridge where you come from?' asked Ma.

'Stop bothering the lad with your silly questions,' cut in Pa. 'Can't you see he's famished?'

'Aye, we do have porridge on Great Island,' I said, 'but it's not as creamy as this.'

She cackled as I gobbled up the last of my food. 'There's more if you want.'

I held out the bowl and she gave me seconds.

'I must get back to the beach the moment I've finished this,' I said. 'Perhaps I'll find my broken skiff washed up on the shore further along from where you found me.'

And then I had a most terrible thought. What if Shadow too had been washed up on that shore? What if he were still alive but injured, unable to walk? That could be the reason why he hadn't come to find me, and here I was eating hot porridge without him.

I tried to get to my feet in a panic. 'My dog,' I cried. 'He might be hurt. I must find him.'

'Oh,' said Ma. 'But you haven't tasted the delicious snails yet.'

'I'm sorry...' I began but my feet gave way under me and I crashed to the ground.

Chapter 10
Prisoner

I woke up to find myself in a dark room. I could see a shadow nearby, framed by a guttering light. Suddenly, it moved.

'Are you awake?' It was Rock.

'Yes,' I said, sitting up. 'I guess I was really tired after my battle through the storm. I fell asleep, I'm sorry.'

Rock came closer. 'You fell asleep because my mother slipped some special sleep herbs in your porridge.'

I tried getting up but something yanked my feet out from under me and I landed on my back. I felt out in the dark and discovered there was a leather rope around my ankle. Someone had tied me up.

'I'm afraid we had to make sure you wouldn't escape,' said Rock.

I felt the blood rush to my head and my cheeks burned. 'What do you mean? Escape from what?'

'From us. You see, Wolf, my family desperately needs an extra pair of hands on the farm. But there is no one to help. No one else lives on this side of the island. It's just Ma, Pa and me. My parents are getting old. Soon they will not be able to work in the fields, or to look after the animals. I will have to do everything on my own.'

'So you thought you'd keep a prisoner to work for you, is that it?' I hissed. 'And you've tied me up like a runaway dog to make sure I don't escape.'

I was tugging furiously on the leather rope, trying to break free.

'I'm afraid you're tied securely to a pole,' said Rock. 'You won't get free.'

'And you won't force me to work for you,' I snapped back. 'I'll escape the moment you untie me to do some work. Or I'll scream for help.'

'There'll be no one to hear you,' laughed Rock. 'No one ever comes here. Now go back to sleep. I need some rest too. We have a hard day ahead of us tomorrow.'

'My people will come looking for me,' I said as Rock unrolled a fur blanket on the other side of the room. 'They'll find me and the shaman will put a curse on you.'

Rock ignored me and snuffed out at the lamp before snuggling under his blanket. I sat in the dark, smarting with anger. But even I didn't believe my family would find me if they came looking for me. This place was remote.

When I heard Rock snoring, I tried loosening the rope from around my ankle. No luck. It was knotted so hard it couldn't be undone. I examined the pole I was tied to. It was wider than a tree trunk and solid as a rock. Finally, I tried creeping up on Rock, praying he would have a flint knife or an axe on him, but the short rope held me back.

Exhausted but still fuming, I sank to the ground. I'd pulled on the rope so hard my ankle was swollen. It hurt. I was so angry with myself for letting strangers trick me, I forgot to pray to the spirits.

Dawn came before I had the chance to go to sleep again. The early morning light shone in through the door. I was being held in the store room. Ma shuffled in to wake Rock.

'You have no right to tie people up as if they were animals,' I shouted. 'I call on the spirits so that they may have revenge on you on my behalf.'

My threats seemed to have no effect on her. She scuttled away without even looking at me. Rock got up and fumbled around, keeping his back to me. When he turned, I realised he had untied the end of the leather rope and strapped it to his own ankle.

'Come on, brother,' he said cheerfully. 'Let's get some breakfast. I'm starving.'

'I'm not your brother,' I snapped.

He shrugged and marched out of the store room, forcing me to hobble after him. Breakfast was more porridge. It was gritty and tasteless this morning. Perhaps it had been the sleeping herbs that had made yesterday's so creamy.

There was no sign of Pa and I noticed that my own clothes had disappeared from the washing stick. I was stuck with Rock's raggedy cast-offs.

We didn't spend too long at breakfast. By the time the morning sun had reached down into the valley, Rock had marched me across the fields to a rocky spot under an ancient tree.

'What are we doing here?' I said.

'We're digging a well.'

I crossed my arms in a show of defiance.

'I'm not digging.'

'No, I'll be doing that. Your job is to scoop away the loose earth and stones.'

'I refuse to do that too.'

'You won't get anything to eat unless you do,' said Rock patiently. 'Do you want to starve?'

I stuck out my chin and said nothing.

Rock shook his head. 'Suit yourself.'

He knelt on the ground and started working away at it with a digging stick. I sat on the ground as far away from him as the rope would allow. I was determined to make his job as difficult as possible.

'Look,' said Rock. 'The quicker we get this well dug, the quicker we can turn to easier work. I don't want to spend the entire autumn digging. So why don't you stop sulking and help me?'

Even if I was still furious, I had to admit his words made sense. Besides, I knew I was never going to earn my freedom just by being stubborn. And I had no chance of overpowering Rock to untie myself. He was twice my size. So I'd made a little plan. I would pretend to make friends with the brute and trick him into untying me. Then I'd run away.

Digging a well was much harder than looking after sheep back home. By midday, my fingers were sore and bleeding and I had blisters on the palms of my hands.

'Come on,' said Rock. 'We've done enough digging for now. Let's go and get some food.'

Over bowls of yet more gritty porridge, I went through my escape plan in my head. First, I would start asking Rock questions about his life, pretending I was getting interested. I bet he was very lonely without anyone his own age in the family or living nearby.

I would open up about my own life, making sure he understood that I too was lonely even if I lived in a crowded village. Once we'd got a bit closer, I'd start dropping hints that I was starting to prefer life on the Island of Red Cliffs, where there was no one to make fun of me.

If I pretended to enjoy the work, to be excited about seeing the well finished, he might just fall for the trick.

Lunch lasted only a short while. Then I was dragged back to the well until the sky turned an alarming shade of yellow. There was going to be a terrific thunderstorm.

'Come on,' said Rock, as it started to rain. 'Let's get out of this wet. It's supper time soon anyway.'

By the time we got back to the farmhouse, I was too tired to eat. I lay on my back in the

storeroom, tied up to that dreaded pole again. Every inch of my body hurt.

Rock and his father sat at the fire pit for a long time, working away at a hide with their scrapers and discussing the well.

'Is the boy asleep?' asked Rock's father.

I pretended to snore.

'He's worn out,' said Rock. 'He's not very strong. I doubt he'll last until we finish the well.'

'Not as strong as the other one, then?' said Rock's father.

'No,' replied Rock. 'We won't get as much out

of him.'

'Perhaps it's all for the better,' said his father. 'I went to see the wise man who lives on the other side of the island this morning. It looks like we're in for a harsh winter. There is going to be severe snow and ice. Our crops will not survive. We will starve unless we offer sacrifice.'

'You mean the new boy?' asked Rock.

'Yes,' said his father. 'As in the ancient days. It will be a full moon tomorrow. We'll take him out to the fields… and bury him alive.'

Chapter 11
The Beast in the Dark

I lay frozen with terror as Rock came to make sure I was still tied securely. He pulled the door to the storeroom shut and I heard the wooden bolts falling into place. With a storm on the way, he must have decided to sleep in the farmhouse.

There was no time to carry out my plan after all. If I was going to get out of this place alive, I had to act fast. But what could I do?

I forced myself to calm down and think but no ideas came. What would the shaman do in this situation, I wondered? He would sing, of course. He would sing the Moonsong.

Well, I would sing too. I would have my own

song, named after me. The Wolfsong.

I started singing, hesitant at first, scared that Rock and his parents might hear and laugh at me. But I soon stopped caring about them and my song got louder. I begged the spirits to come to my rescue, to free me. I sung with feeling, with passion, until I had to stop because my throat was sore.

By now the wind had died and I became aware of a loud scratching noise outside the storehouse. I sat bolt upright, shaking with fear. Had my loud singing attracted a hungry wild animal? Was something monstrous trying to get in?

The sound was coming from the back wall and I stared at it even though I could see nothing at all. I knew the wild animal was ripping through the dried mud and straw with its paws. Soon it had made a hole big enough for moonlight to stream through.

I caught a flash of fast-moving paws, of sharp claws. Then the beast squeezed through and I heard it leaping across the storeroom towards me.

It dropped something at my feet and growled.

I recognised that growl at once and my heart nearly stopped. I hardly dared talk.

'Shadow? Is it you? Are you alive?'

Shadow answered with a soft whine and I felt his warm tongue lick my knee.

Joy and relief flooded through me. I went down on my knees and opened my arms in welcome. 'Shadow, it is you,' I cried. 'You brave dog. You survived the storm, and now you have found me. You *are* my guardian spirit. And what gift have you brought me?'

I felt around the floor and my hands closed over a flint knife.

Ha, Shadow was so clever. He had just *known* what to bring me. It took only moments to hack myself free while Shadow skipped happily around me. He bounded to the hole in the wall and I squeezed through after him, bringing half the mud wall down behind me.

It was still raining but we ran without even looking back. I shouldn't have been able to take more than a single step after my hard day at the well but I think joy and the thought of freedom gave me strength.

Shadow and I pelted across the muddy fields and past the newly-started well. I followed my beloved dog along the valley and round a rocky headland overlooking the beach.

Shadow stopped outside a small cave partly hidden with slimy boulders. He barked.

'Hello?' A boy in a fur cloak came to the entrance. He looked surprised to see me but also, I thought, pleased. 'Oh, welcome,' he said. 'Are you the dog's owner? Are you hungry? I have crabs roasting in the fire. It's nearly ready.

'The name's Sparrow, by the way. What's yours?'

Chapter 12
Spirit Brothers

'I'm Wolf,' I said.

'Pleased to meet you, Wolf. Come in.'

I could see how the boy had got his name. He was short and squat, like a bird, with a small round head topped with feathery hair. One look at his arms and legs, though, and you realised that first impressions can be wrong. He rippled with muscle.

Sparrow grinned and walked back into the cave. Now I could see a warm, inviting fire inside but I still hesitated. Having just escaped from one trap, I wanted to make sure I wasn't stepping into another.

Shadow seemed to have no such doubts. He trotted into the cave after Sparrow and gave his knee a friendly lick. He had obviously made friends with him and trusted him. I followed.

'I found the poor thing half dead on the beach,' said Sparrow, giving Shadow a hug. 'His stomach was full of water but I managed to pump it out. Does he belong to you?'

'His name is Shadow,' I said. 'Our boat was smashed to pieces during the storm.'

'He must love you very much,' smiled Sparrow. 'He was too poorly to even walk yesterday but he seemed to get better very quickly. He must have come looking for you the moment he could. He took one of my flint knives too. He is so clever.'

Sparrow handed me a chunk of steaming meat on the end of a stick. It smelt delicious. Before I took a bite, I tried to give Sparrow his knife back but he refused. He said it sounded like I needed it more.

'I was kidnapped by two farmers,' I said between huge bites. 'They held me prisoner on a farm in the valley behind the cliffs. I spent the whole of yesterday helping to dig a well.'

'Rock and his father,' said Sparrow.

'You know them?'

'I was their prisoner too, until they forgot to snuff out the lamp one night. I used it to burn through the rope and here I am, hiding in this cave until I can get off this island.'

'Oh, I think I heard Rock's father mentioning you,' I said. 'Are you not from this island, then?'

'No, I was born on High Island, three days' from here, but there was a raid on our village and I was taken prisoner. The raiders sold me to Rock and his father. Now if only I could get off this island and back to mine.'

'How long have you been in hiding?' I asked. 'Why did you not build a boat?'

'I am a farmer's child. I have no idea how to make a boat that will carry me away safely,' replied Sparrow.

'Ha, I have the skills to make a fine skiff,' I said. 'You can help me and we'll escape together. I was on my way to Seal Island before the storm blew me here.'

'High Island almost touches Seal Island,

although it is much smaller and very few people live there,' cried Sparrow. 'What good luck.'

'Luck has nothing to do with it,' I laughed. 'It is the work of the spirits. They are helping us.'

'And it is the result of kindness,' said Sparrow. 'I saved your dog and now you are saving me.'

'Look, the rain has stopped and the moon is out,' I said. 'Let's waste no time. We'll start looking for driftwood right away. We'll need some dried hides too.'

'I have plenty of those,' said Sparrow. 'I learnt to dry hides by watching Rock's mother. But are you not tired after working hard all day and then running all the way here?'

'I should be,' I said, 'but I want to get off this island as quickly as possible.'

Sparrow stopped at the cave's mouth. 'Wait! We are putting our lives in each other's hands. Let's swear an oath by the hidden spirits to never betray each other. It's what my people do before they start an important project. Give me a lock of your hair.'

I used the Sparrow's knife to lop off a bit of my hair. Sparrow did the same with his own hair. Then he rolled the two tufts into a ball between the palms of his hand. Carefully, he placed it into the fire and within moments it burnt away into nothing.

'Now our spirits have mingled in the smoke of the sacrifice,' said Sparrow. 'We are one in the eyes of the spirits – Spirit Brothers.'

Chapter 13
Seal Island

We heard Seal Island through the fog before we saw it. It was almost dark and the island's famous seals had come ashore for the night.

It had taken Sparrow and I two days to build our skiff, keeping a lookout for Rock and his father in case they came looking for us. It took us another day to carve our paddles. But now we had left the Island of Red Cliffs behind and were approaching what I hoped would be a welcoming shingle or sandy beach.

Shadow barked ferociously and the seals' honking stopped immediately, if only for a few moments. Perhaps they had never heard a dog barking before and imagined it was some terrible monster. We dragged the skiff up onto the beach.

'Let's hide it behind that large rock over there,' said Sparrow. 'We'll sleep under it. It's not safe to go knocking on people's doors at night.'

We dragged the upturned skiff behind the rock and I covered it with seaweed while Sparrow made a bed under it. Even if the fog lifted while we slept, it would be hard to spot.

During our journey, I had explained to Sparrow why I had left home in search of Seal Island, and what I hoped to take back with me.

'The locals might turn nasty if you accuse one of them of stealing a sacred object,' said Sparrow. 'We'll have to pretend we are here for another reason. I remember my father saying this island is well known for its hard-wearing pottery. Perhaps we could pretend we've come to barter for storage jars.'

'That's a brilliant idea,' I said.

In the morning, I picked some limpets which

we had for breakfast. Then we set off along a well-trodden path that took us to the top of a steep hill. We came to a village that looked very much like my own, although the houses were not connected with covered corridors.

'It seems to be quite a large place,' I said to Sparrow, 'but there are very few people about, and no one has given us a second look. When strangers arrive in our village, someone talks to them right away, to find out if they're friendly or hostile.'

'I agree, it's very strange,' admitted Sparrow.

'Let's go to the meeting place,' I said. 'We're bound to find someone bartering there. Perhaps they'll tell us what's happening.'

We followed an old lady carrying a large grass basket and within moments came to a market surrounded by stone huts. Most of them were shut and had bleached skulls stuck in the grassy roof.

'Ram heads,' I said. 'Their horns are meant to keep away evil. The folks who live in those huts are scared of something.'

A few people were milling about, well-wrapped in furs and sheepskins. Shadow barked and bounded towards one of them, his tail wagging joyfully.

'Why, Shadow,' said a voice I recognised at once. 'How did you get here?'

It was Crow.

She turned and saw me. A big grin spread across her face and her green eyes flashed with happiness. There was no flicker of guilt about what she'd done, no trace of shame.

'Wolf,' she cried. 'What a surprise. When did you get here?'

She took a step towards me and I noticed she was limping. She had a crutch under her cloak.

'I came in a skiff with my friend Sparrow,' I said. 'What happened to your leg?'

'Ha, I nearly got home in one piece from your island. But my boat was caught in one of the treacherous currents around Seal Island and I was thrown ashore. My boat was smashed to pieces and I landed on a jagged rock. I broke my leg. It's only these last few days I have been able to start walking again, although it'll be a long time before I can do any running or hunting. Still, I survived and I am grateful to the spirits for it. It must be the necklace your mother gave me.'

She opened her cloak to show me the blue beads around her throat. 'Your mother was right. They did protect me.'

Chapter 14
Crow

I stared at the beads. If they were still around Crow's neck how had Rain found them outside the tunnel in our burial mound?

My head swirled with confusion.

'I need to get back home,' said Crow. 'My leg is starting to hurt. Come with me. My father will be pleased to see you. I have told him a lot about you and your village that has no chief. Your friend can come with us.'

'This is Sparrow. He comes from High Island,' I said. 'I'll tell you how I met him when we get to your home.'

'I look forward to hearing your story!'

Crow led us past more houses with sheep skulls in the roof.

'What is happening here?' I asked.

'The spirits have put a curse on this island,' explained Crow. 'People are dying mysteriously and no one knows why, not even the shaman. Now many are too scared to even leave their house. No one is working the fields or making pottery.'

We came to a stone house, the first one I had seen on Seal Island with the door open.

'Father?' called Crow. 'Are you back from the fields?'

There was no answer and we trooped inside.

'Please, take off your cloaks and sit close to the fire,' said Crow. 'I'll cut us some dried meat.'

'I should explain why I came to find you,' I said while we ate. And I told her all about the stolen spear and the blue beads Rain had found outside the burial mound.

'I do not blame you for suspecting me,' said Crow graciously when I finished. 'But I assure

you these beads have never left my neck.'

'And you could hardly paddle all the way back to Great Island and dig into a burial mound with a broken leg,' added Sparrow.

'Ha, but I could have sent someone in my place,' said Crow. 'Which I didn't. Still, I'm ashamed to say I might be responsible for your spear going missing just the same.'

I put down my food. 'How?'

'Sparrow, close the door so no one will hear us,' instructed Crow. 'And both of you come closer.' She poked the fire and started:

'When I came home to Seal Island, my father held a feast to celebrate my homecoming. Only the most important people in the village were invited because my father is the chief and usually only village elders are allowed in our house. One of them was the shaman. I remember he listened very carefully to my story, especially the bit about seeing the burial mound outside your village. He made me repeat everything you said to me, about the skeletons inside and the healing spear.

'A few moons later, a lot of people in our village started to get ill and die. Nobody knows why still. One day they would be healthy and the next, they would fall over in a faint and get sick. We offered sacrifice to the spirits, we held special dances round the fire but it was no use. People kept on dying.

'One night, the shaman came to see us. He gave me a gift of healing potions for my leg but now I realise that was just an excuse to get more information out of me. He brought up the subject of my journey to your island again and asked me a lot more questions, especially about

the healing spear.

'The very next morning the shaman left Seal Island on a journey of his own. He said he was going to live alone on a deserted island for a while, to be at one with the spirits and find out why so many of us were dying. A lot of people had started questioning his powers and he was determined to save his reputation.

'But now I am sure he did not go to a deserted island. He must have travelled to your island and stole the healing spear from your village instead. Imagine, if its powers worked and people stopped dying, our people would start looking up to him again.'

'But you said people are still dying,' said Sparrow.

'I think perhaps the healing power only works when the spear is in the hands of its rightful owner,' said Crow.

'But what did your shaman do with the spear?'

'He probably placed it in our burial mound,' replied Crow.

'Then we must demand he hands it over to me,' I said.

'Don't be silly,' said Crow. 'No shaman is going to admit he broke into a burial mound and stole a dead man's possessions. As you know, stealing from graves is frowned on by both spirits and people. You two will have to break into the burial mound yourselves.'

Chapter 15
Inside the Burial Mound

I could see Sparrow turning pale at the suggestion. 'Will the spirits not curse us if we do that?' he asked.

'You won't be stealing,' explained Crow. 'Wolf will only be taking back what rightfully belongs to his people. Just make sure you don't tread on any bones. *That* is meant to bring bad luck.'

There were footsteps outside and a tall man in a sheepskin cloak appeared at the door.

'Welcome home, Father,' Crow got up on her crutch. 'These are my friends. Wolf is the boy from Great Island I told you about. Sparrow lives on High Island.'

'It is an honour to meet you both,' replied Crow's father. 'Make yourselves at home. Sadly, I can't stay. I only came home to fetch some food. The shepherds out in Chestnut Valley need my help. Now the sheep have started to fall ill. There's no end to this nightmare. Crow, don't wait up for me. I might not be able to come home until the morning. And make sure you bar the door properly before you go to bed.'

He left with a hunk of dried meat wrapped in cloth. The rest of us waited until it got dark and I found once again that I could talk to Crow as if I'd known her my whole life.

The village was eerily silent as we left the house, Crow carrying a lit lamp. No one was about and the sheep skulls stared at us from the grassy roofs. Shadow did not like them and growled every time he saw one.

We came to the burial mound which looked very much like the one outside my village, except that it was much bigger and higher. The wind ruffled the grass on it and made a wild, moaning sound. It gave me the creeps.

'How are we going to break in?' I said. 'We haven't thought this out properly.'

Crow didn't reply. She limped around the rim of the mound, looking closely at the grass.

'Here it is,' she said at last.

I hurried up to her. 'What have you found?'

Crow was pointing to a small bush growing out of the mound. I pushed the branches aside to find a round flat stone blocking a small hole.

'That's a secret tunnel in case the shaman gets trapped in the burial mound during one of his secret rituals,' she said.

'How did you know about it?' I asked.

Crow smiled. 'I discovered it a long time ago, playing on the mound. Oh I know it's forbidden, but I was only little.'

'It's not going to be so difficult getting into this place after all,' I grinned. 'You hold on to Shadow, Crow. I don't want him coming in after us.'

But getting into the burial mound was not as easy as I imagined. First, we had to drag the heavy stone aside. Then I had to worm my way through the tunnel, sharp stones tearing at my furs. Thick cobwebs brushed against my face and a hairy spider skittered down my neck. When I finally climbed out into the tomb, it was pitch dark and something crunched under my feet. I hoped I hadn't stepped on human bones already.

Sparrow climbed in after me, bringing in the torch.

We had come out in a narrow corridor with doorways on either side. At the far end was a chamber with a platform in the middle. Lying on it was a skeleton still wrapped in old furs. He was surrounded by large clay pots. I guessed they held all the things he'd used in his life. He must have been very rich and powerful to own so much. Perhaps he had been a chief or a powerful shaman.

'Be careful how you go,' I warned Sparrow. 'We need to get to that important skeleton and we

don't want to step on any bones.'

'There are skeletons inside these doorways too,' whispered Sparrow, his voice husky with fear. 'They're everywhere. Some of them are wearing bangles on their wrists, and necklaces.'

'But I have a feeling we only need to get to *that* man with the clay jars,' I said.

I was right. When we got to the skeleton, I could see he had a spearhead in his hand. The shaft, carved with dolphins and deer I vaguely remembered, was gone. Maybe the shaman from Crow's village had removed it to hide the spearhead under his cloak. But even so, as Sparrow held the torch closer, I knew it was my village's spear.

'I'll get it,' said Sparrow.

He reached out with his free hand but he couldn't wrench it from the skeleton's grip. It was stuck fast.

'Let me try,' I said.

I reached out and the spearhead came away in

my hand the moment I touched it. Almost at once, I felt something – an invisible force – run up my arm and flood through me. It made the hairs stand on the back of my neck.

The feeling remained only a few moments, but while it lasted I saw a gushing spring in a valley. There were dead sheep lying on the grass around it. I could see right to the bottom of the water and something really hideous lying in the mud.

Chapter 16
I Find Me

'Did you get it?' asked Crow as I wriggled out of the tunnel.

'Yes,' I said, 'and I discovered something else too: the reason why your people and animals are dying. There is a dead serpent at the bottom of the spring that feeds your river. It is poisoning your drinking water. Perhaps if you remove it, all will be well.'

'How did you find that out?' asked Crow, looking amazed.

'I think the healing spear showed me,' I said.

'But if the spear showed you,' whispered Crow, 'that means you must have special magic powers. The spear didn't show our own shaman anything. Perhaps you are one of the few people who can truly make the magic of the spear work.'

I shook my head. 'Me? Magic? I don't think so.'

And yet, when Crow told her father about my vision, he took some men to the spring right away. They discovered the dead serpent at the bottom of the spring, just as I had said.

I would have loved to stay on Seal Island a few more days, to see if people stopped getting ill. But Sparrow was eager to get home, and Crow thought we should leave before the shaman found out that someone had broken into the burial mound. I had to agree with her.

She came down to the shore to see us off.

'Promise you will come and see me when your leg is better,' I said.

'I will,' promised Crow, 'I am sure I will have good news about my people. And I shall bring Sparrow with me.'

'I would love to see Great Island,' said Sparrow. We got into the skiff and Crow threw an earthenware pot into the sea as an offering.

The spirits must have been pleased with it because we got to High Island without any more mishaps. I said goodbye to Sparrow on the shore, knowing he would want to be alone with his parents when he got back home.

'You will get the healing spear back to your people safely, won't you?' he said as I checked the skiff over before heading out.

'I shall guard it with my life,' I promised.

'Then goodbye, Wolf.'

'Goodbye.'

The journey back to Great Island gave me lots of time to think. I'd always felt uncomfortable in my skin, not knowing what the future held for me.

And all the while, the signs had been there. My parents calling me Wolf, after the mysterious creature of the night. My ability to tell good stories and to sing. Shadow appearing out of nowhere to be my spirit guide. My fondness for just staring at the sky and the sea, wondering what mysteries they were hiding!

None of it had made sense until that brief moment of magic in the burial ground. Now, with Crow's words fresh in my mind, everything was clear. I knew that all those gifts had been sent by the spirits to help me become a special person in my community.

A healer! I would heal not only broken people and bones, I would also heal broken spirits. I had set out to find a stolen spear and in the process, I had also found me.

There was still one small part of the mystery I hadn't solved. Did Rain know the beads he had found outside our burial ground were not Crow's? And if he knew they were not, why had he lied?

But that was a question that must be answered some other time, in another adventure. As I beached the skiff close to the Shark's Teeth, Shadow leapt up to the path to the village.

Mother heard us coming and came out of the door. Father and Hawk came out behind her.

'Wolf,' she gasped, and she pulled me into her arms. 'Thank the spirits you are home safe and sound.'

'Yes, thank the spirits,' repeated Hawk.

'I brought the stolen spear with me,' I managed to say in between hugs. 'It's safely home too.'

'You have done well, my son,' said Father as he gently took the spearhead. 'I am proud of you. You are a credit to this family and the village. We shall have a great feast in your honour and you shall tell us all about your journey.'

And for the first time I could remember, Father actually *smiled* at me.

Wolf's journey will continue in

The Whispering Stones

HiSTORiCAL NOte

The Stolen Spear is a work of fiction. It is set at the end of a period we call the Late Neolithic, around 2500BC. Man had largely stopped being a wandering hunter and had learnt to grow crops, keep farm animals and live in communities. It was the end of the Stone Age and the beginning of the Bronze Age when people started to use metal for tools and weapons.

All the characters in the story are made up, although I like to think that they behave as Neolithic people did. The locations are based on true places but I have not given them the names we use for them today because that's not what Stone Age people would have called them.

Wolf's village is now known as Skara Brae. It's on the Western coast of Mainland, the largest island in the Orkneys in Scotland. It was inhabited from around 3180BC to 2500BC when it was mysteriously abandoned and left to fall to ruins.

The spooky burial mound outside Wolf's village is based on a real one, also on Mainland. Today it's called Maeshowe. Experts consider it one of the finest Neolithic burial grounds in the world. Together with Skara Brae it has been designated a UNESCO World Heritage Site.

I drew on information about another burial mound in Mainland, the Unstan Chambered Cairn, to describe the cairn on Seal Island.

Hoy, the second largest island in the Orkneys, was the inspiration for the Island of Red Cliffs. You really will see red cliffs if you go there. They are some of the highest cliffs in the U.K. If you visit you might also spot a strange tall rock standing at the coast like a massive pillar. It's called The Old Man of Hoy. It didn't exist in the Stone Age but was formed by natural erosion in the 18th century. However, it inspired me to use a similar rock in my story.

Crow's and Sparrow's islands are largely made up although in my mind's eye they are based on real ones today called Flotta and Fara.

The serpent in Wolf's vision was inspired by a strange carving on a stone believed to be from Neolithic times. It was found near Loch Ness and shows a mysterious serpent-like creature.

The necklace that Wolf's mother gives Crow is also based on some beads found scattered in one of the Skara Brae houses. They were made of bone and animal teeth. Perhaps they were part of a bracelet or necklace. Who knows who wore them in Neolithic times?

DISCUSSION POINTS

During Wolf and Shadow's adventure, **friendship** plays a key role. It is something that is vital to us even now, thousands of years later.

- How do the friendships change in the book?
- Why is friendship important to the characters?
- When do we see the power of friendship?

The Stolen Spear is full of twists and turns. There are many things that we **discover** as we read the story.

- What discoveries do we and Wolf make?
- How do ways of life differ from island to island in the story? How does Wolf discover this?
- What do we learn about the characters as the story goes on?
- What does uncovering mysteries teach us about the world?

Change upturns Wolf's previous way of life, but it also helps him see a new side of himself.

- How do other characters experience change?
- How do they feel when they go through change?
- What different changes does Wolf go through?
- Why is it imporant for Wolf to experience this?

The **late Neolithic era** was a period of great change but it was still very different to our way of life.

- What part of Neolithic life were you most surprised at and why?
- How can we see the shift from the Stone Age to the Bronze Age in *The Stolen Spear*?
- Why do you think spirits held such importance to the Neolithic people?
- Are there any similarities between our modern way of life and the Neolithic people's?

Wolf meets many different people during *The*

Stolen Spear, and there are **different points of view**. Some are kind and some are cruel.

- How does seeing things from someone else's point of view help us understand their actions in the story?

- Are there any points of view that you agree with, or disagree with? Why?

- Which characters try to see everyone's point of view?

In order to find the spear, Wolf must find his **courage**.

- Where is Wolf courageous in the story?

- Are there any other characters who are courageous?

- What does *The Stolen Spear* teach us about courage? Where does it come from?

ABOUT the AUthOR

Saviour Pirotta is a children's author who loves myths and legends but also detective stories, mysteries and adventures. He has written many kinds of books, including pirate stories, non-fiction and, more recently, detective stories. He particularly likes writing historical fiction.

Saviour grew up on the island of Malta, which is home to some of the world's most fascinating prehistorical sites. As a child, he made up characters who would have used these temples and villages. Wolf and Crow were the children in these fantasies and the *Wolfsong* series gave him the opportunity to share them with the world.

We asked Saviour some very important questions:

If you were stuck on a desert island, what item would you want to be stranded with?

A book, of course, or at least a set of books, namely The Chronicles of Narnia.

What's your favourite time period?

I don't have a particular favourite. I love the Stone Age, Ancient Sumer, Mesopotamia, Egypt, Greece and Rome, and the Victorian era too.

If you had a super power what would it be?

To be able to read four books at the same time.

What's your favourite colour?

Light blue. It reminds me of the sea.